Street Luge

John Nichols

Raintree Steck-Vaughn Publishers

A Harcourt Company

Austin · New York

www.raintreesteckvaughn.com

Published by Raintree Steck-Vaughn Publishers, an imprint of Steck-Vaughn Company.

Library of Congress Cataloging-in-Publication Data
Nichols, John, 1966-
Street luge/by John Nichols.
p. cm.-- (Extreme sports)
Includes bibliographical references and index.
ISBN 0-7398-4692-2
1. Street luge racing--Juvenile literature [1. Street luge racing.] I. Title. II. Extreme sports (Austin, Tex.)

GV859.82 N53 2001
796.6--dc21   2001019863

Printed and bound in the United States of America
1 2 3 4 5 6 7 8 9 10 WZ 05 04 03 02 01

Produced by Compass Books

Photo Acknowledgments
Kent Kochheiser/KK Photo.net: All photos except;
Alex Schelbert, 36

Content Consultant
Darren Lott
Author of *Street Luge Survival Guide*/ ESPN X Games medalist

Contents

Introduction

S treet **luge** is an extreme sport that is growing more and more popular. Street lugers race light sleds down courses at high speeds. Extreme sports are relatively new sports taken up by daring athletes. Along with the fun of extreme sports, however, comes the risk of injury. People who participate in extreme sports must do everything they can to be safe.

You have probably heard of the **X Games** and the Winter Olympic sport of luge. But how did street luge begin as a sport? How is it related to skateboarding? Who are the top street lugers and what are the top street luge competitions in the world today? What do you need to do if you want to take up the sport? This book will answer all of these questions and more.

This is pro street luger Pam Zoolalian wearing a helmet and a leather suit for protection.

How To Use This Book

This book is divided into parts called chapters. The title of the chapter tells you what it is about. The list of chapters and their page numbers appear in the Table of Contents on page 3. The Index on page 48 gives you page numbers where you can find important topics discussed in this book.

Each chapter has colorful photographs, captions, and side-bars. The photographs show you things written about in the book, so you will know what they look like. A caption is an explanation that tells you about the photograph. The captions in this book are in light blue boxes. Side-bars give you extra information about the subject.

You may not know what some of the words in this book mean. To learn new words, you look them up in a dictionary. This book has a dictionary called a glossary. Words that appear in boldface type are in the Glossary on page 44.

Street luger Dennis Derammelaere, in orange, goes so fast he sometimes leaves the ground.

You can use the Internet sites listed on page 46 to learn more about topics discussed in this book. You can write letters to the addresses of organizations listed on page 46, asking them questions or to send you helpful information.

At the start of a race, pro street luger Dave Auld uses his hands to build speed.

Street Luge

S treet lugers ride paved roads or paths at high
speeds. They ride a special kind of skateboard or
sled called a luge. They lie down on it on their back
and ride feet first. Luges are also called sleds.

Street luge has its roots in skateboarding and luge.
Luge is a sport similar to bobsledding done on ice
tracks. It is a Winter Olympic sport. Many street
lugers joke that their sport was invented by a tired
skateboarder. They say that this skateboarder lay
down on his board and rode it down a hill.

Street lugers race each other in races that may
feature as few as two and as many as 24 riders. After
each run, some of the riders are eliminated. The
lugers that are left race again. They keep racing until
there is one winner. The riders steer through courses
that twist and turn. They can reach speeds up to 80
miles per hour (128 kph).

What Safe Lugers Do

Safe street lugers never ride alone. It is important to have another person along in case of an accident. Young lugers should make sure their parents or guardians know what they are doing.

Safe lugers never ride where it is against the law to luge.

Safe lugers check their equipment for wear. Wheels and other parts must be replaced regularly. Worn equipment can be dangerous.

Safe lugers wear full face helmets at all times.

Safe lugers cover every part of their bodies so they do not scrape their skin. Most street lugers wear a suit made of leather. They make themselves easy to see. Many wear bright clothes and reflective tape that can be easily seen even when there is not much light.

Safe lugers check their route before riding to make sure it is safe. This includes making certain there is no traffic.

Safe lugers never choose a route that is too difficult. A smart luger picks a route that is challenging and fun but not impossible or dangerous.

Safe lugers use a **chase car** to protect them from traffic. The car can also give them a ride back up the hill.

Safe lugers obey the rules of the road. Speed limits are not just for cars. If riders go faster than the speed limit, they could get a ticket from the police.

Beginning street lugers should practice on courses with no traffic. Turning, braking, and stopping are skills to be learned before a rider goes on a route with traffic.

> At the beginning of race, safe street lugers make sure that every racer knows the rules.

What is Street Luge Like?

Luge is the French word for "sled." Street luging is like sledding without snow or ice. Courses can be made on any paved path or road that goes downhill. For this reason, street luge is referred to as a "gravity sport." The Gravity Games are one of the most important street luge competitions.

 Street lugers lean in order to turn.

Safety Gear

It is important that lugers wear safety gear, including **helmets** and protective clothing. They reach very high speeds. Without protection, they could be injured or even killed. An injury is some kind of hurt or damage, such as broken bones or a sprain. A sprain means one of the body's joints has been twisted, tearing its muscles or ligaments. A ligament holds together the bones in a joint.

The danger of street luge is why many people like it. They like the thrill of racing down a course with the road just beneath them. Some people say that street luge is too dangerous. Others say it is dangerous only when riders are not properly trained or do not use the right safety equipment.

Different Kinds Of Street Luge

Riders have found different ways to keep their sport fun and challenging. One kind of luging is called endurance luge. Endurance is the ability to work hard for a long period of time. Some endurance riders compete to see who can ride the most miles in a set period of time. The set time is usually 24 hours. Other endurance riders try to ride a certain distance in a set period of time. Riders must use the same sled and equipment until they finish, break down, or quit.

Did You Know?

Did you know that many lugers go hunting for old tires? They cut them apart and attach the treads to the bottom of their shoes. The thick tread helps them stop quicker. It also protects a luger's feet better than shoes alone could.

This car is making sure that no traffic enters the route pro luger Darren Lott is riding.

Other Kinds of Luging

Another kind of luging is called night luge. Riders attach battery-powered lights to their helmets and boards so they can luge at night. One reason they do this is because there is usually less traffic at night. Riders with lights and reflectors at night are easier to see than are riders during the day. All night lugers must wear lights and clear shields on their helmets. If they do not, they could crash and be seriously injured.

Dirt luge is another kind of luging. These lugers ride dirt roads in the country instead of paved roads in the city. Dirt lugers use bigger and softer wheels to go over the bumpy ground. Riders are able to slide easily on the loose dirt.

How Street Luge Began

No one knows for sure when street luge began. It was probably invented by skateboarders in the 1970s. They sat or lay on their boards and rode them down steep hills.

Timeline

Early 1970s: Skateboarders lie down on their boards to ride them

1975: First Signal Hill Speed Run

1995: The X Games holds a street luge event.

2000: First place lugers win $15,000 at the Gravity Games; street luge event winners get $10,000 in prize money at the X Games

Signal Hill Run

In 1975, a series of skateboard races were held at Signal Hill Speed Run in southern California. Some racers stood up on their boards and some lay down and some lay down and also rode headfirst. The racers reached speeds of 60 miles per hour (97 kph) or more on the short, steep track. The racers who had lain down went the fastest, so more riders began to try that method.

After 1978, the Signal Hill races were canceled. Yet the idea of street luging as a sport had been born. Today, thousands of riders compete in events around the world.

Luger Profile: Biker Sherlock

Michael "Biker" Sherlock has won more medals than any other racer in street luge history. He was born in New Jersey in 1968. By 2000, he had won seven X Games medals and five medals at the Gravity Games. He started riding in street luge in 1995 and won his first X Games medal in 1996. He is president and owner of Extreme Downhill International (EDI) which sponsors and regulates downhill skateboarder and street luge events and competitions.

This luger has lost control during a race.

Getting Started

A street luger's most important piece of equipment is the luge. They can be made from wood, aluminum, steel, or fine threads of glass called fiberglass. A headrest holds the rider's head up and makes it easier to see. There are pegs or a footrest where riders can put their feet.

The most experienced riders usually use luges that are 8 feet (2.4 m) long and very light. On the bottom of the luge are skateboard-type **trucks** and wheels. Trucks are the frames that hold the wheels to the luge. On street luges, trucks move when the riders lean to one side or the other. Riders turn the luge by leaning. Wheels on a street luge are made from a material called **urethane**. Riders have to change the wheels often because of wear.

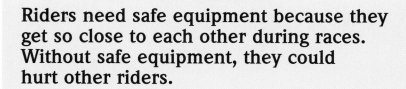

Riders need safe equipment because they get so close to each other during races. Without safe equipment, they could hurt other riders.

Wheels and Clothing

When going fast, the wheels on a street luge will go around about ten thousand times per minute. The heat caused by the friction of the wheels on the street can cause the wheels to melt or explode. Sometimes the wheels melt in the middle of a race and then will not work properly. Almost every rider has experienced a wheel failure.

Lugers need equipment to protect themselves. Riders should always wear helmets and gloves. Beginners should make sure each part of their bodies is covered. Experienced lugers recommend that every rider wear elbow and knee pads. Experienced riders who go fast wear special shoes, gloves, and suits made of leather, called **leathers**, to keep them safe.

Luger Profile: Dennis Derammelaere

Dennis Derammelaere has won five medals at the X Games. As of 2000, only "Biker" Sherlock had won more. Derammelaere retired from street luge after winning a gold medal in the 1999 X Games. A few months later, he returned to the sport. A pro since 1995, his nickname is "D-Rom." He was born in California in 1973.

A luger's equipment includes a helmet
and thick gloves and shoes.

Street Courses

A smoothly paved, steep road is the best street luge
course. It must be steep enough so riders can build
speed. It must long enough to make the ride last. A
typical course is from one-half mile (.8 km) to four
miles (6.4 km) long. Some luge runs are more than 10
miles (16 km) long. There must be room at the end of
the course to slow down and stop safely.

All lugers will crash. That is why it is safest to ride only on protected courses.

Safe Courses

Streets used for luging must be free of traffic. There should be few or no other streets that cross the route. Friends should stand at cross streets to warn riders if traffic is coming. If they are not sure that they can stop traffic, then they should not ride the course. They could be injured or killed. The safest riders block off courses to keep out traffic before they "drop a hill," or take a ride. They must ask the police if they can do this. Lugers often try to find a street like this that ends in the parking lot of a business that is closed.

Street lugers should always have a friend follow them in a car. The friend can prevent other cars from hitting the luger. This is called using a chase car. The chase car can also bring the luger back to the top of the course for another run.

Lugers on city streets must obey the laws of the road. They need to obey street signs. They should never get in the way of traffic. Riders who do not obey the laws could get a ticket, get injured, or even killed.

Did You Know?

Did you know that street luge made it into the *Guinness Book of World Records?* The 2000 edition of the book lists a rider named Tom Mason. He rode a street luge faster than anybody else ever has. Mason's official world record for speed on a street luge is 81.1 miles (130.5 km) per hour.

Pro luger Biker Sherlock is about to race on a special course where all traffic has been blocked off.

Race Courses

Riding on special race courses is the safest way to luge. Traffic is blocked off on these courses. Large bricks of hay and straw called bales are placed around these courses to create bends and turns and to protect riders if they crash.

Most race courses are shorter than street courses. They are from 1/2 mile (.8 km) to 1 mile (1.6 km) in length. They are different shapes and sizes. Some have many twists and turns. Riders cannot go as fast on these courses. They test a rider's ability to control a sled. Other courses are straight so riders can build speed.

Because as many as 24 people race at once, it is important that racers follow rules to avoid accidents. They cannot touch other racers or their sleds to steal speed from them. Doing this is called "mooch bumping." They cannot get in the way of racers trying to pass them. Rough riding is not allowed

Professional lugers teach beginners that the safest place to ride is on a course that is closed off from the dangers of traffic.

Who Can
Become A Street Luger

When they ride, street lugers are very near the pavement. They can feel every bump in the road. They need to be able to respond quickly to what they see or feel. They do not necessarily have to be very big, fast, or strong, but they do need to be in good physical shape.

A safe street luger must be able to control his or her sled at high speeds. Beginners do not need to go fast to enjoy the sport. Even speeds of 20 miles per hour (32 kph) can be fun for a beginner. With the right training and equipment, street luge is a sport almost anyone can enjoy.

Skills To Learn

Riders turn their sleds by leaning to one side or the other. Any amount of leaning can make a sled turn. Riders must learn how much or how little to lean.

Street luges have no brakes. Riders use their feet to control their speed. They drag the heels of their shoes along the ground to slow down. This is why they wear thick-soled shoes to protect their feet.

Sliding is a way to make a sharp turn when you are going too fast. To slide, riders lean to one side and drag a foot. The wheels skid while they turn and help

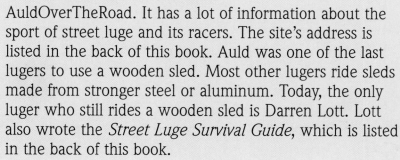

Luger Profile: Dave Auld

Dave Auld has been one of the top street lugers since the early 1990s. He was born in New Jersey in 1964. His Internet site is called AuldOverTheRoad. It has a lot of information about the sport of street luge and its racers. The site's address is listed in the back of this book. Auld was one of the last lugers to use a wooden sled. Most other lugers ride sleds made from stronger steel or aluminum. Today, the only luger who still rides a wooden sled is Darren Lott. Lott also wrote the *Street Luge Survival Guide*, which is listed in the back of this book.

These riders are braking coming out
of a turn on a closed-off course.

the rider slow down. This turns the sled faster. Sliding
should only be done by experienced riders.

Riders must learn how to crash properly. Falling
properly can keep you from being injured. When
falling, riders try to keep their bodies flat and their
hands and legs spread out. This slows them down and
prevents them from flipping over or rolling.

Where Do I Train?

Street luge is still a new sport. There are not as many places to train as there are for other sports. Routes are often busy with traffic. There are very few courses used just for street luging. Most street lugers learn how to luge by riding as often as they can. They practice on routes they find on their own.

There are a few groups that help beginners learn the sport. One of the largest groups is called SLED. SLED stands for Street Luge Education and Development. At SLED classes, beginners learn skills and safety from some of the top riders in the sport. If you want to contact SLED, its address is listed in the back of this book

There are also hundreds of private street luge clubs all over the world. Beginners can join them and learn from more experienced riders. You can contact SLED, or other organizations listed in the back of this book, to ask them to help you find these clubs.

Most professional lugers, like Lee Dansie above, are happy to teach beginners the safest and best ways to ride.

Professional street lugers compete against each other on safe, dry tracks.

Who Are the Professional Street Lugers?

Professional street luge is a very new sport. A professional athlete is someone who gets paid or earns money for competing in a sport. Street luge pros are not as well known as other sports stars. They can make money from their sport, but only a few earn enough to make a living. Most have other jobs and race for fun.

In the United States and Canada, pro street luge competitions are usually held in the summer months. There are about 20 major events in a pro season. The good weather and dry tracks found in the summer are important for safe luging.

The very best pro street lugers earn money from **sponsors**. A sponsor is a company that pays a rider to use or advertise its product.

What Does it Take to Be a Pro?

Most pro street lugers are men between the ages of
25 and 40. Of the top 200 pros, only one is a woman.
Her name is Pam Zoolalian. Because there are so few
women pros, she often competes against the men.

"I enjoy competing against the guys," says
Zoolalian. "It is a challenge, and this sport is all about
challenging yourself." Most of the men she races are
stronger and heavier than Zoolalian. This make them
faster on the straighter parts of a course. Zoolalian's
small, light body allows her to turn more quickly than
most men.

Bob Pereyra is one of the best male street lugers in
the world. He began riding around 1984. He has
given himself the nickname "Piranha." A piranha is a
fish from South America that has been known to
attack and eat people and large animals. Pereyra chose
this nickname because he is a fierce rider.

Pereyra is one of the pioneers of the sport. "I love
the speed," says Pereyra. "I'm proud to be one of
the first street lugers and I think our sport has a bright
future." Pereyra wrote many of the rules for street luge
racing. He is still one of the best riders in the world.

Riding the Street

At the top of the course, riders always check their equipment to make certain that it is working properly. Then they sit up on the luge and signal the chase car to begin. To start, riders reach down and push off the ground with their hands. Once they build speed, riders lay down. This helps their bodies cut through the air and go faster.

Street lugers wear protective clothing to keep from getting injured in accidents.

Controlling a Luge

Beginning riders often stare at objects they are afraid they will run into. They should not do this. Their body and the sled will usually go in the direction they are looking. This could cause the rider to crash into the object he or she is trying to avoid. A good lesson for a new rider is to look where you want to go, not where you do not want to go.

Riders usually reach top speed in the middle of a course. Smart lugers know not to go faster than they can handle. Crashes happen when riders try to do too much. Riders must lean only enough to turn or direct the sled the amount they want. Even a slight tilt of a rider's head can change the direction a sled is going. Too much of a lean makes the sled spin out. Not enough of a lean makes the sled not turn enough. The rider could miss the turn and crash.

At the end of a route, riders need to slow down and stop. To stop, they drag their heels along the ground and sit up at the same time. The luge gradually comes to a stop.

Dropping a Hill

A professional street luge race has as many as 24 people racing at the same time. Riders have to stay in marked lanes for a set distance from the start. After that point, they can "**blend**," or ride the course any way they like. As they pick up speed, racers must be careful not to touch other riders or their sleds.

One skill racers use is called **drafting**. To do this, one racer follows closely behind another. The racer in front cuts through the air for both sleds.

Professional and beginning street lugers gather at competitions around the world to watch the best lugers control their sleds at high speeds.

Competing in Street Luge

There are several groups that run the sport of street luge. They set the rules for events and also set the rankings for pro racers.

The two groups that run almost all of the major street luge events are the International Gravity Sports Association (IGSA) and Extreme Downhill International (EDI).

Competitions and Prizes

Pro street luge competitions are held all over the world. The two biggest competitions are the Gravity Games and the X Games. These are shown on television and have events in several different extreme sports. The X Games are sponsored by the sports television network ESPN.

A rider must be at least 16 years old to enter a professional street luge race. Riders who are under 16 can enter special events for juniors or for amateurs.

Major Events

In the late 1980s and early 1990s, there was little prize money to be won in street luge competitions. The winner of a race would win as little as $50. Today, prize money is much better. At the 2000 Gravity Games, the winner received $15,000. In the 2000 X Games, the winner of an event received $10,000.

Only the top racers are invited to the X Games and the Gravity Games. Lugers have to earn the right to enter them by qualifying. Qualifying means they win or do well in enough other races to earn a spot in a major event.

Luger Profile: Pam Zoolian

Pam Zoolalian is the only woman ranked among the top 50 riders in the world. She is one of about 20 female pros. She wears hot pink from head to toe and enjoys beating many of the best male riders. The only woman to ever earn a spot in the Gravity Games, she has been ranked as high as 10th in the world. She has been luger since 1996.

Future of the Sport

Street luge is one of the fastest growing sports in the United States. In only a little more than 20 years, it has grown from being a skateboarder's hobby to becoming a sport known around the world.

Lugers are trying to make it easier for others to try the sport. New **luge parks** are being planned and built around the country. These are safer than riding on city streets. At parks, beginners can learn without having to share a course with traffic.

Street lugers are also working to make better equipment. They want to build sleds that are faster, safer, and easier to steer. Many street lugers hope that some day their sport will be included in the Olympics.

Did You Know?

Do you know what buttboarding is? Buttboarding is like street luge, only it is done on regular skateboards. Street lugers can reach higher top speeds than buttboarders, but they cannot turn as quickly. On a twisty course, the fastest buttboarder will beat most street lugers. You can learn more about buttboarding at the "Buttboarding.com" Internet site listed in the back of this book.

Quick Facts About
Street Luge

A hill is steep enough to street luge on if a car can reach the posted speed limit while coasting down it.

Street luge made its first appearance at the X Games in 1995.

The name "street luge" was created by the sports television network ESPN.

A rider must be at least 16 years old to enter a professional street luge race.

The wheels on a street luge are measured in millimeters. Most are from 70 mm to 127 mm (2.8 to 5 inches) tall.

Cut and scrapes on the skin are the most common way that street lugers get injured.

In an official race, all street lugers must wear full-face helmets. These helmets cover a rider's whole head and face and have an opening that allows the wearer to see. The opening is usually covered with a clear or tinted windshield that can be raised or lowered.

Glossary

blending (BLEND-ing)—when street luge racers are allowed to leave their set lanes and use any part of a course

chase car (CHAYSS KAR)—a car that follows a street luger along the route to protect the luger from traffic

draft (DRAFT)—to follow closely behind another racer in order to gain speed for a pass

helmet (HEL-mit)—a hard kind of hat that protects a person's head

leathers (LETH-urz)—full body suit made of leather

luge (LOOJH)—the French word for sled; also a medal sport at the Winter Olympics done on a toboggan called a luge, which is usually made of a fiberglass shell mounted on two steel runners with curved wooden tips.

luge parks (LOOJH PARKS)—courses made especially for street lugers to ride free of automobile traffic

professional (pruh-FESH-uh-nuhl)—a person who makes money doing something others do for fun

sliding (SLIDE-ing)—to turn a luge sharply by leaning and dragging a foot

sponsor (SPON-sur)—a company that pays someone to use what it sells or to advertise its product

truck (TRUHK)—a metal frame that holds wheels and moves as a rider leans

urethane (YUR-uh-thayn)—a hard material used to make wheels

X Games (EKS GAYMZ)—a popular extreme sports competition hosted by the sports television network ESPN

Internet Sites and Addresses

AuldOverTheRoad
http://www.
auldovertheroad.com

Buttboarding.com
http://www.buttboarding.com

**Extreme Downhill
International**
http://www.
downhillskateboarding.com

Gravity Games
http://www.gravitygames.com

**International Gravity
Sports Association**
http://www.geocities.com/
ozmans_streetluge/
IGSAInfo.html

StreetLuge.com
http://www.streetluge.com

**Extreme Downhill
International**
1666 Garnet Avenue, PMB #308
San Diego, CA 92109

**International Gravity
Sports Association**
638 North Crestview Drive
Glendora, CA 91741

SLED
18734 Kenya Street
Northridge, CA 91326

X Games
ESPN Television
ESPN Plaza
Bristol, CT 06010

Books to Read

Lott, Darren. *Street Luge Survival Guide*. Irvine, CA: Gravity Publishing, 1998. This book discusses all aspects of the sport of street luge, including its evolution, equipment, methods, and current practice. Written by one of the sport's pioneers, it also profiles top riders, lists professional organizations, and focuses throughout on safety.

Ryan, Pat. *Street Luge Racing*. Mankato, MN: Capstone, 1998. This book introduces the history and development of the sport, discussing it as a sport that combines skateboarding and ice lugeing.

Index

DATE DUE			

796.6
NIC

Nichols, John.

Street luge

FRANKLIN ELEMENTARY SCHOOL
MEDIA CENTER